Yellow Line

Sylvia Olsen

orca soundings

ORCA BOOK PUBLISHERS

National Library of Canada Cataloguing in Publication Data:

Olsen, Sylvia, 1955-
Yellow line / Sylvia Olsen.

(Orca soundings)
ISBN 978-1-55143-462-9

1. Native peoples--Canada--Juvenile fiction. I. Title. II. Series.

PS8579.L728Y44 2005   jC813'.6   C2005-904420-9

First published in the United States, 2005
Library of Congress Control Number: 2005930529

Summary: The line separating Native and White begins to blur
for Vince as he finds himself falling for a First Nations girl.

Orca Book Publishers gratefully acknowledges the support for its publishing
programs provided by the following agencies: the Government of Canada
through the Book Publishing Industry Development Program and the Canada
Council for the Arts, and the Province of British Columbia through the BC Arts
Council and the Book Publishing Tax Credit.

Cover design by Lynn O'Rourke
Cover photography by Getty Images

ORCA BOOK PUBLISHERS
PO Box 5626, STN. B
VICTORIA, BC CANADA
V8R 6S4

ORCA BOOK PUBLISHERS
PO Box 468
CUSTER, WA USA
98240-0468

www.orcabook.com
Printed and bound in Canada
Printed on 100% PCW recycled paper.

12 11 10 09 • 6 5 4 3

In memory of Jerry Matkin

Before I start

Where I come from, kids are divided into two groups. White kids on one side, Indians, or First Nations, on the other. Sides of the room, sides of the field, the smoking pit, the hallway, the washrooms; you name it. We're on one side and they're on the other. They live on one side of the Forks River bridge, and we live on the other side. They hang out in their village, and we hang out in ours. In the city they are called First Nations; out here they've always been called Indians, and we don't change stuff like that in a hurry.

Neither village is much to talk about. Ours is bigger than theirs, but altogether there are less than 500 people. Highway 14 passes through. Fifteen minutes to the west is the wharf, the Raven's Eye Pub and Lodge and the ocean. An hour and a half or so to the east is the city. It has the police station, the high school, the Salvation Army, a post office, a real grocery store and even a McDonald's. It's more like a grubby little hick town than a city, but it's better than our dump of a village.

Whichever way you drive, the highway is a twisting logging road full of potholes. The only reason they fix the potholes is so that the tourists will come out to hunt and fish or check out the ocean and beaches. Nobody in the city cares about our village. The fact is, hardly anyone even knows it exists.

The separation thing works like this. When Indian kids are on our side of the bridge they hang out at the gas station. White kids hang out just up the road and on the other side at Ruby's, your standard dingy smokes, pop and chips kind of store. They walk on one side of the road. We walk on the other. It's like there's a solid yellow line down the middle. Their side of the bridge is the Indian reserve. There is a No Trespassing sign on the road, so no white kids go down there.

There's a yellow line on the school bus as well. It divides the front of the bus from the back—us at the back, them at the front. You can't see the line, but everyone knows it's there and no one crosses over. It's just the way it is, and as far as I remember it's the way it's always been. Ninety minutes to school and ninety minutes back, and no one steps a foot in the other territory. Except Dune.

Twenty minutes into the trip to school, on the straight stretch between the hairpin turn and the beach cliffs, the bus pulls around the corner and there's Dune. He's walking down the middle of the road. I don't know where he lives. There's nothing around—no telephone lines, no driveways—just forests and clear-cuts. Every morning Dune hops on the bus and plunks his butt down dead center. Behind them and in front of us. But then, with his black hair, white skin and green eyes, no one knows for sure whether he's one of them or one of us. According to the stories people tell, Dune and his mom live in a log shack that's so close to the beach, surf laps right up to their front door. Some people think he belongs to one of the Indian guys. Other people think his dad is one of the men from our side. Either way he's probably somebody's half brother.

All the men out our way are loggers or fishermen, or at least they were when there was work. Dad is one of the few guys who still works in the bush. Most people are old or unemployed.

Dad says there used to be a bowling alley, a restaurant and a basketball team. Now the place has shriveled up like a dried prune full of old people and weirdos who have escaped from the city. The one thing that's stayed the same, Dad says, is that people have always known their place. Indians on one side and whites on the other.

Dad says right out that he hates Indians. Mom smacks her lips and rolls her eyes and pretends she doesn't agree.

"Haven't you heard of equality and tolerance, Jack?" says Mom. "This is the twenty-first century. They're no worse than whites—just different."

But then Mom didn't grow up in the village like Dad did. She says she's urban, and in the city people of different races mix with each other all the time.

"Where I come from," Mom preaches, "we're all just human beings."

That might be what she says, but it's not how she acts. Mom's been around long enough to feel the same way as Dad, just not long enough to say it out loud. For instance, she makes sure she's on the other side of the road when she sees an Indian coming. And when the women in the village started a committee to get a separate school bus, who do you think was the spokesperson? Mom, of course.

This is what our village is like. Or *was* like. Dad and Mom are pretty much like everyone else. I was the same as them. We all lived by the rule of the yellow line. Us and them. Them and us. It's probably hard to believe a village like ours actually exists unless you've lived here. And if you've lived here all your life, like I have, you still might have trouble believing it. But then again, I changed and maybe our village will change too.

Chapter One

The bus rolls up to Ruby's at 7:05. We pile in, file past the front seats and spew into the rear half of the bus. I throw my legs across the bench seat. Nick and Justin sit across the aisle.

The back row is usually reserved for guys in grade twelve, but this year there are none. That leaves the grade elevens— me, Nick and Justin—sole residents for two years. The row ahead of us belongs to Sherry, the only grade-eleven girl, and a couple of miscellaneous grade-ten girls. Sherry and I have been neighbors since we were born. Our parents are friends and we're like brother and sister, which completely sucks because Sherry is hot. It happened this summer. She went to visit her cousin in the city—old, plain-Jane Sherry. She comes home three weeks later. Boom, she's transformed. One instant we're brother and sister; the next instant she's steaming hot and I'm salivating. Now she is too good for me.

I toss my backpack behind my head. I'm ready to close my eyes when I notice Sherry sits three rows up, one row behind the row of separation, next to Millie, her little sister. Two things are wrong with this scene. The first thing is Sherry's not sitting in front of us, and second, she never talks to Millie. When I look at her I can see there's a third thing. She's peering

Sylvia Olsen

around like she's expecting someone to show up. The bus jerks forward, twists around the corner and then stops at the gas station—the Indian bus stop. They have the same priority ranking system as we do. Oldest on first and the youngest up front behind the driver. With Sherry acting so weird, I figure I better keep one eye open. When Steve gets on the bus, I sit up a little and take notice because he's the next thing that's unusual this morning. He's a big guy, grade twelve, plays rugby, a little shorter than me, but bigger. At six three, I'm the tallest guy in the school. But there's no doubt that Steve is the biggest guy at Rocky View High School. He has forty or fifty pounds on me and carries it around like he's wearing football equipment. From the scars on his face, he looks like he's been in a few dustups. It's not like I spend my time gawking at the guy. I've just noticed a few things from getting on the same bus with him for eleven years.

Steve usually stumbles on the bus hanging his head like he's half asleep and then falls into the last row of Indian seats. But this morning he's standing straight up with his hair pulled back in a pussy ponytail, and he's all cleaned up like he's going somewhere special. He scans the back seats until he lays his eyes on Sherry and then shoots her a look, up and down, and stalls in the aisle as if he's deciding where to sit. I drag my butt up a little higher to get a better look.

Finally Charlie, Steve's younger brother, shoves over and Steve hauls into the last row of Indian seats. That's not the end of it. Steve hunches up so he's half facing the back of the bus. I'm thinking he's looking for trouble and, sure enough, the look he shot Sherry's way was no mistake. He's eyeballing her.

Suddenly I'm ready to blast out of my seat and sink my fist into his face like I caught him messing with my mother. I'm ready to go, man. Then I'm thinking, wait until he buries himself, one more move, then I'll hammer him.

Steve's got it coming. He's the kind of guy who doesn't know his place. At school he's the man. Most of his friends—other than a few Indian guys and this chick—are rich white kids from town. He was voted the most popular guy in the school. Dad says Steve is the only Indian with that distinction. But on the bus, or at least up until now, he's minded his own business.

Pretty soon I see Sherry swinging her legs around sideways so she's half facing Steve. I can't believe what I'm looking at. She's got her eyes plastered on him and a sloppy smile on her lips.

The rules of separation in our village are clear and everyone knows them. The most important rule is: Date your own kind. Mom says that people in the city date anyone they want, no matter what color they are. Not in our village. Dad says there are a few guys who married Indians and live over there. But there are no mixed couples living on our side.

I try to keep an eye on what's going on. "Sherry," I call. I talk normal, like I have something to say to her.

She doesn't hear.

"Hey, Sherry," I call again.

She turns around and throws me a look as if to say I'm interrupting her.

"What?"

"So what's up?" I say, just trying to break their stupid spell.

She shakes her head as if she can't hear me. Feeling like an idiot, I shrink down into the backseat.

Before I disappear, Steve shoots me a look like, *What a moron.*

Sweat is beading up on my forehead, and I want to jump out of the seat and pound the crap out of the guy.

Chapter Two

By the time we get to the school, I can hardly sit still.

"Hey, man." Justin drags himself to a sitting position. "Are you in some kind of hurry this morning?"

I'm pushing kids out of my way and keeping my eyes on Sherry at the same time. I finally catch up to her in the parking lot.

"Hey," I say casually. "What's up?"

"Huh?" Sherry throws me a *Who are you?* look.

"How are you doing?" I try again.

"Fine."

"What are you doing?"

"Going to class, stupid," she says. She's treating me like I'm an idiot who's trying to make time with her. She's right, in a way. It's not like I haven't thought about getting my hands on her.

"Yeah. Of course."

She runs ahead to Steve.

"Hey." I hear her silky voice. "What's *his* problem?"

My ears are ringing like church bells, and my feet feel like they are buried in concrete. The burning sensation has changed into a cold sweat. My body and mind are a mass of confusion. Sherry and I used to jump off the bus together.

"I'll see you around," I mumble to no one in particular.

Justin and Nick catch up with me.

"She's too hot for you now," Nick laughs. "That girl sure scrubbed herself up in a HOT bath."

"No freaking kidding," says Justin. "Now even Mr. Basketball ain't good enough for her."

That's the thing. I mean, it's not like I'm a nobody—I'm a Hoop Hero. Grade eleven and I'm already provincial athlete-of-the-year material. I'm the captain of the school basketball team, and last year I was the highest scorer on the senior team—first grade ten to do it. We took the pennant. Provincial champs. And who was the MVP? Vince Hardy—like they say, Mr. Basketball. And who was at every game cheering for me? Sherry Porter.

"Shut up, Justin," I snap. "Like I give a rat's ass. Sherry's like my sister, man. I'm just looking out for her."

"Yeeaaah," chirps Nick. "Who the hell does Steve think he is?"

"You guys should have seen them when you were sleeping," I say. "Eyes all over each other."

"No way he's moving in on her, man," says Justin. "She's the hottest chick this year."

Inside the school, Sherry's leaning against her locker, eyeing Steve. He's flexing his muscles and pumping his chest. Without talking, Nick, Justin and I form a line shoulder to shoulder, me on the locker side. We stride past them. I catch Steve off guard and give him a solid body check from behind. Perfect. He stumbles against Sherry and into the locker. With the speed of a fighter, he swings around and grabs me with both hands. Instantly a crowd forms in the hall. Nick and Justin, like the wimps that they are, take off down the hall. I'm left dangling from Steve's arms.

"Vince," Sherry says, "you used to be so cool."

Steve drops me like a hot potato. While he was holding on I was scared, but once I'm free I'm instantly raging.

"Get your hands off me," I shout in his face.

"If you know what's good for you, you'll leave me alone," Steve says matter-of-factly. Then he turns to Sherry and says, "Don't worry about him."

What the hell is going on? Since when does he need to tell her not to worry about me?

Nick and Justin reappear as soon as the crowd disperses and they realize I'm not going to get murdered.

"Hey, Vince," says a voice.

I glance around. The little Indian chick who follows Steve around is left standing where the crowd was.

"It happens," she says. "Don't sweat it."

Chapter Three

"Pass," I shout.

The basketball season opener is in two weeks and our team sucks. All the good players, except for yours truly, graduated last year, leaving a few decent players and a bunch of rookies.

"Vince!" Coach Baker waves me over to the bleachers. "You're the leader this year. We need more than baskets.

We need motivation." He slaps my back. "What's wrong with you today? Pick it up."

"Vinny. Vinny." Girlie voices interrupt him. Charlie and a bunch of guys from the reserve are standing at the gym door. "We're counting on you, Vinny. You're our man."

I can't see who's got the smart mouth.

A girl shouts, "Hey, white boy, you sure got hairy legs."

"Vince, keep your eye on the ball," Coach Baker yells as I jog back onto the court.

"Look at his spider legs," the girl hollers again. "He looks like he just crawled out of a cave."

"Vince," calls Nick. "Where's your game, man?"

I shake my head. The only thing I can think about are the taunts coming from the huddle of losers.

"Looks like he's gonna break," someone by the door says. There is an eruption of giggles.

I wheel around to take a look at them and smash face first into the wall. They are laughing their guts out like they've just seen the funniest thing in the world.

"Hey," Coach Baker finally shouts at the crowd. "Either suit up or get out of the gym."

"Losers," I shout, regaining my balance. "Shut your freaking mouths."

My nose feels like it's expanded to the size of a grapefruit.

I keep hollering at them as they push their way out the door. "Get the hell out of here before I throw you out."

Suddenly they stop and form a line across the doorway.

"You gonna throw us out, white boy?" Charlie shouts. "Come on. Let's see you try."

Like a choreographed dance group, they step onto the basketball court. They form a semicircle around me. Out of the corner of my eye I see two massive guys moving toward me. I dodge backward in time for Coach Baker to grab my shirt and drag me out of their reach.

"I told you guys to get out of here," he shouts. "I don't want to see you in the gym again unless you want to play."

"Later," shouts Charlie. "We'll get you later, Hardy."

I throw a shot in his direction. "Later," I yell. "I'll be there."

"Chicken," a girl shouts as they walk out the door. "He's got chicken legs with black hairs! Yuck."

"Settle down, Vince." Coach Baker shoves me back onto the bleachers. "Listen to me, boy. If I catch you fighting those guys anywhere near this school, you're going to be sitting on the bench. I don't care how many baskets you get. This team is respectable. No fighters."

"Chicken Legs." I can still hear the girl. "Your legs need to be plucked."

I clench the edge of the bench and hold on until my knuckles turn white. I'm pumping with a crapload of energy like a freaking maniac. If my hands bust loose, I'd be down the hall in an instant, busting a few heads.

Chicken Legs.

The words scream around in my brain. My nose is throbbing. Losers. They're all losers.

Suddenly my eyes take a quick unplanned look at my legs. They're long and white and scrawny and covered in a coat of thick black hairs, with knees attached in the middle like knobby potatoes on skewers. They shock me. I mean, they're so ugly I want to puke.

"Tomorrow, Coach," I shout. "I'm finished today."

I grab my towel and race into the showers.

Chapter Four

When I get on the bus after school, I feel terrible. My fists are clenched like I'm a tough guy. But the truth is, I'm terrified. That's how you feel when you're a pathetic weakling and a gang of tough guys promises to kick your ass.

"Keep looking over your shoulder, white boy," says one massive guy. "We're ready to beat the crap out of you."

Charlie kicks his boot into the aisle, making like he's going to trip me, and says, "Better keep your eyes open, white boy."

"Good thing you got your pants on," says a girl as I pass. "I'd cover up too if I looked like you."

She should talk. I'm about to tell her she's an ugly little mutt when I notice she's sitting next to the girl who was standing in the hall. Her eyes meet mine just as I'm ready to let fly. She shrugs and smiles as if to say, *I don't think they're very funny either.*

I keep my mouth shut and stumble past. I collapse in the backseat.

"We can take those guys," says Nick.

"Yeah. We'll storm them at the gas station." Like a tough guy, Justin shouts to Manny and Turner, who are sitting a few seats in front of us. "You guys want to meet us at the gas station? We're going to teach those morons a lesson or two."

Manny and Turner will be no help whatsoever. They're brothers and both in grade eight. Although they've been in grade eight for a few years, so they could be older than me. "Shut up, Justin," I say. "I'm not fighting anyone."

"What? You're going to let them treat you like that?" Nick is getting frustrated with me.

"No," I say. But I'm thinking yes. I'm a weakling, an unplucked chicken. Those girls are right. I'll get annihilated if I try to fight those guys. And Nick and Justin? Forget it. They're as skinny as me. None of us have ever been in a fight. We've pushed a few guys around a bit, but this thing threatens to be a major rumble—something totally out of our league.

"We'll get them," I mumble unconvincingly. "Just not right now."

I intend to disappear off the face of the earth. I slump in the seat and plan how I can melt into a puddle.

After a few minutes, I raise my head and catch a glimpse of Steve and Sherry. Steve's in his usual seat and Sherry's two rows behind. Both are sitting sideways facing each other and smiling and talking. They're not even pretending to ignore each other. Strictly speaking they're sticking to the seating rules, but I can feel the lid is about to blow off. Sherry's acting like Steve's her boyfriend. The worst part of it is she looks like she doesn't think there's anything wrong with it.

Charlie's butt is hooked on the edge of the seat next to Steve. He's turned sideways with his legs in the aisle and is looking my way.

"Vinny," he shouts. "He's our man. Maybe today, maybe tomorrow.

We're coming after you. You are going to be one sorry little white boy."

He turns around. He faces the front of the bus, holds his middle finger up in the air and shouts, "Here's to you, Vinny."

I want to ignore everyone, but my eyes keep straying in the direction of the girl who talked to me at school. She's turned slightly my way. When I throw her a glance, I get the feeling she's looking at me. I try to ignore her, but the next time I look I catch her eyes and she smiles. There's no doubt about it. She smiles at me. She has big white teeth and full lips painted red. It's the kind of lipstick that makes you want to eat her lips alive. Her eyes are round and turn up a bit on the sides. She looks soft and friendly when she smiles, not like anyone else on the bus.

I quickly look away in case she starts to giggle with the rest of the girls. Why is she being friendly? What's she up to?

The next time our eyes meet, I smile back. Am I out of my mind? I want to grab my smile and stuff it back in my face. What am I doing? I sink down into the seat and close my eyes. I can't get my mind off her lips and her eyes. I can still see her smile.

She's an Indian. Mom and Dad would freak if they knew what I was thinking. What difference does it make anyway? When Charlie and the gang get their hands on me, I'll be dead meat. My eyes stay closed until the bus hauls up to the Indian bus stop.

"Later, Vinny, my man," I hear Charlie shout.

"Sometime," a voice hollers. "You'll never know when."

Another voice says, "We'll be looking for you."

Through the mass of voices and giggles I hear, "Chicken Legs. You need to be plucked."

The bus door closes. I drag myself to a sitting position. Steve is the only Indian left on the bus. He stands up, but instead of getting off, he moves to the seat vacated by Dune. He is directly in front of Sherry. She leans on the back of the seat and talks softly. She can have him. They deserve each other. He can sit right on top of her for all I care. Go for it, Steve. Wait until I tell my parents and they tell Sherry's. They'll take care of you, big guy. But then I realize I don't care about any of that anymore. It's not about Steve and Sherry. It's about Charlie and the rest of the morons who are going to smear my body into the gravel and throw what's left of it into the river. And the worst part is, it's not just them. I can't stop thinking about the girls staring at me and giggling.

Chicken. Chicken Legs.

What the hell is wrong with me?

Then I notice the Indian chick from the hall is still sitting in her seat. Why didn't she get off at the Indian bus stop? She walks off with Steve when the bus stops at Ruby's and waits next to the bus until I jump off the stair.

"Don't worry about those guys, Vince," she says. "They're morons."

Then she throws me another smile and I melt.

"Hey, sweetie," says Nick. "You waiting for me?"

"Shut up," she says. Then she turns and faces me. "My name's Raedawn. I'm Steve's cousin."

"*Ooohhh*," Justin butts in. "Steve's cousin. Tell Steve he better watch out because we're after him."

"Get out of here, Justin," I say.

She smiles again and turns away.

"She's a nice piece," he says. "Even if she does live over the bridge. Nice little piece of ass."

"Shut up, you pig," I shout. "Just shut up."

It's not only Nick and Justin I want to shut up. I want the whole world to shut up. I want everything to slow down so I can figure out what the hell is happening to me. Instead of going to Ruby's, I turn up the path and run all the way home.

Chapter Five

Since Ronny, my older brother, moved away three years ago, meals at our place are dead boring. Mom sets the food on the table. Dad sits at one end, Mom at the other and I sit between them on the side of the table that faces the wall. I keep my head down, eat and get out of the kitchen as fast as I can. Mom and Dad talk about logging,

Dad's boss, Mom's friends or who said what to who. It's always the same stuff. Nothing happens in our town, so conversations tend to be recycled news from days or weeks before. If something does happen, like when the Owens had a party and Mr. Owen got so drunk that he fell down the stairs, then, like instant messaging, the whole town knows the details in a matter of minutes.

I sit down, ready to shovel spaghetti onto my plate, and Mom says, "Vince, I hear there was a ruckus on the bus today."

I've been home for less than an hour and she already knows everything.

"Huh?" I pretend I don't know what she's talking about.

"I hear the Indian boys were threatening you," she says.

"What the hell did you say?" says Dad.

"Nora phoned and said that she over-heard Justin and Nick saying that the Indian boys are after Vince."

"No way," says Dad. "Those damn Indians better keep their hands off my boy."

"And Vince didn't do a thing to provoke them," says Mom.

They keep on talking as if I'm not in the room. "Of course he didn't do a thing. I've told Vince since he was a kid to stay away from the Indians," says Dad.

"And they said something about Sherry and one of the Indian boys," says Mom.

Once Dad realizes he needs more information, he remembers I'm in the room.

"What the hell is she talking about?" he says.

I think about playing dumb. But then I get the urge to let Sherry pay for the way she's been treating me lately. Maybe she'll remember I'm her best friend when Steve is out of the picture.

"Yeah," I say. "You know Steve. I told you about him. He's the rugby player, the one who got voted the most popular guy in the school."

"Hell, yeah, I remember," says Dad. "So what?"

He's itching for me to make a big announcement. Mom's eyes are almost popping out, she's so interested in what I have to say. I think again about shutting up. But if I tell them about Sherry and Steve, it's bound to deflect their attention away from what happened to me on the bus. "Well," I continue, "they're getting it on."

"What the hell do you mean, getting it on?" Dad's busting an artery.

I'm thinking of how to describe getting it on when he shouts, "What the hell do you mean, Vince? Are you telling me some Indian guy is sleazing around Donnie's little girl?"

Mom pipes in, "Poor Sherry. She needs to be careful."

"So what the hell are you doing about it?" says Dad, like this suddenly is my problem.

"Me?" I say. "What *can* I do about it?"

"If some Indian is after Sherry, you better make sure he doesn't get his hands on her," says Dad. He's shoveling spaghetti into his mouth like he's a garbage disposal.

"Who said Sherry doesn't like it?" I say.

"What did you say?" says Dad. He puts his fork down and points his finger at me. "Sherry doesn't like it, son. I know Sherry doesn't like it. She's the daughter of Donnie and Deb, and she knows better than to like it. That girl has been brought up the right way. She knows to stick to her own."

"Is that the problem you had on the bus?" asks Mom. "Did you stick up for her?"

"Whatever, Mom," I say. "I don't want to talk about it."

Mom and Dad don't understand one thing about me. It is like talking in a windstorm. Words fly around in every direction, and when you're finished you feel like no one heard a word.

"You better talk about it, son," says Dad. "No girl of Donnie's is going to be hanging around with a damn Indian. She's been looking grown up lately, and now they're following her around like a pack of dogs."

I pick up my plate and head downstairs to my room in the basement.

"Vince," calls Mom. "Vince, you need to talk to us. We can help."

I shut the door.

Before Mom finishes her spaghetti, she'll be on the phone with Deb, Sherry's mom, telling everything. Dad will be heading next door before he cracks his next beer to tell Donnie his version. With some satisfaction I think that will be the end of Sherry and Steve.

The next day, Sherry arrives late at the bus stop.

"You loser, Vince," she snarls at me. "You think you can ruin what me and Steve have by telling your mom and dad? What kind of baby are you?"

She barges in front of me and stomps up the stairs into the bus.

"I don't care what anyone says," she says over her shoulder. "I'm with Steve. Get used to it."

At the next stop, Steve gets on and walks straight through the dividing line. He just strides down the aisle as if he's done it every day of his life and plunks himself next to Sherry. In one move, he blows away years of school bus seating arrangements.

The truth is, the reason I'm fuming has nothing to do with where they're sitting. I'm choked because Sherry's treating me like a moron. No one else on the bus cares where they sit either. Charlie and the gang of reserve guys don't seem to notice. The bus pulls away, then immediately grinds to a halt and the door opens.

"Hurry up, Raedawn," says Alice, the bus driver. "It's not like you to be late."

"Sorry," says Raedawn. "I had to print something on my computer and it was ornery this morning."

My stomach gets a fuzzy-peach feeling when I hear her voice. After she settles in her usual spot, she turns around and looks directly at me. She gives me a little finger wave and then faces the front of the bus.

"Did you see that?" says Nick. "That chick thinks you're cute, Vinny. She's waving at you."

"Say hello to the little girl, Vinny," shouts Justin, loud enough for everyone to hear.

I want to punch him in the face. I want her to know I think he's an idiot. I get this urge to ask her where she got a cool name like Raedawn. Then I remember she's not one of us. I sit back and think about her lips and her smile. Something has gone seriously wrong with me. Why can't I get her out of my head?

"They all want you, Vince," laughs Nick. "The guys want to kill you and the girls want your legs, man. They love you. They love your legs."

"Shut up," I say. "Just shut up."

Chapter Six

If trouble is supposed to come in threes, then I'm way overdue for it to stop. Threats from Charlie and the gang, insults from the girls, stupid tough-guy stuff from Nick and Justin, lovey-dovey BS from Sherry and Steve, and Mom and Dad are talking to the whole village. Steve and Sherry are the biggest news in a long time. Then there's Raedawn.

She watches me like she's hunting. She shows up when I'm not expecting and quietly keeps her eyes on me. When she says hi, my stomach feels like I've swallowed an orange. When she's not around, I think about her eyes and her lips and that's not all.

On the bus on Friday afternoon, I keep my head down. It's a long shot, but I'm thinking that with any luck I can get through the weekend without all hell breaking loose.

"Vinny, how does tonight sound? At the river? Under the bridge. Be there." It's Charlie.

The bus stops and the Indians head down the stairs.

"If you're not there, Vinny," he says, "we'll come and find you and it'll be worse."

Steve stands up as if it's the first he's heard of their threats and says, "Leave him alone, Charlie."

"Hey, man," says Charlie. "This ain't got nothing to do with you, bro. This is between him and me."

"No, it's not," Steve says. "It's about me and Sherry. So leave it alone."

Charlie stands up next to Steve. He only reaches his brother's shoulders, but he's built like a linebacker.

"You can have your white chick. But this idiot's not going to push us around. That's my business."

Steve sits down and says, "I'm telling you, Charlie, leave him alone."

"Tonight." Charlie ignores Steve and shouts, "Be there or else, Vinny. Eight thirty."

"We'll be there," says Nick.

Justin spurts out of his seat. "We're ready for you morons."

"Shut up," I say. "They're not after you guys."

The bus takes off with Steve and Raedawn still in their seats. She's waiting when I get off the bus.

"Don't go down to the river," she says. "Stay home. They won't come looking for you if you stay in your village."

"We're not afraid of those morons," says Justin. "We'll be there."

She ignores him, looks me in the eye and says, "I mean it, Vince. Don't go down there."

She turns to Justin and says, "You're a bit of a moron yourself. And if you know what's good for you, you'll stay home too."

He lunges toward her and I pull him back.

"Come on," I say. "Leave her alone."

"What's with you these days, Vince?" says Nick. "Does that girl have something on you? You're acting like a loser."

Raedawn disappears.

At six thirty, Justin and Nick bang on the basement door. They barge past me and into my room.

"Hey man, we got a twenty-sixer of Canadian Club from Nick's place," says Justin. He pulls a bottle out from under his coat, cracks it open and chugs. "Have some, Vince. You're going to need it for tonight."

I hold up my hand and say, "I pass, man. I'm not going tonight."

"No way. You can't not show. They'll come looking for you here," says Nick.

"Then they'll have to find me here. I'm not going," I say. I surprise myself by how sure I am. If this had happened a few weeks ago I would have drunk the bottle, downed a few beer and been waiting at the river for those idiots to arrive. I would have made sure all the white boys in the village were there as well. But that was before I became a world-class weakling. It wasn't Charlie's threats that changed everything. It was those girls and all their stupid comments. They crawled under my skin and sucked out all my confidence. *Chicken Legs, you need to be plucked.* Forget being the Hoop Hero or Mr. Basketball. I'm a real coward.

That's not all that's changed. For one thing, I just don't care about Steve and Sherry like I used to. The new improved Sherry looks good, but she's a hag. I sort of feel sorry for Steve. He's got himself into a hell of a mess, and he just doesn't know it yet. The other thing is Raedawn. When I'm not obsessing over getting killed, I'm obsessing about her. If she's going to be down at the river, there's no way I'm going to get massacred in front of her. I'd rather be called a wimp.

Nick grabs my jacket and throws it at me.

"Come on, let's go," he says. "If we get there early we can figure out a strategy."

I toss my jacket back.

"I said I'm not going. We aren't going to win, guys. There will be at least ten of them and three of us. "

"What's with you, man?" says Justin. "You're the basketball star. You're the man. Since when have a bunch of Indians freaked you out?"

"Since I don't want to get killed."

"Whatever, man," says Nick. "We can take them. Let's go down there and work it out. They'll arrive all half cut and we'll be ready for them."

"Forget it," I say. "You're already half cut. And we aren't ever going to be ready for them. They play rugby. Remember? We play basketball. Strategy isn't going to do us any good tonight."

Nick and Justin pass the bottle back and forth a few more times until they empty it.

"You sure?" Nick says.

"Yeah, I'm sure." And the drunker they get, the surer I become.

Justin rolls off the bed and leans against the wall. "No problem, Vinny. We'll take care of them."

When they finally stagger out the basement door, I lock it behind them. I realize that I used to be that stupid.

The empty feeling in the house creeps me out. It's like I'm ten years old and wish Mom and Dad were home. I take the stairs two at a time, lock the front door and close the windows. When I get back to my room I lock the door, shut the window and flop on my bed. I grab the controls to the video game and gawk at the screen. My plan is to keep my eyes on the game until the flashing and buzzing and popping numbs my brain.

It works. Pretty soon the only thing left in my head is Raedawn. I can see her crouching behind the bushes near the bridge. She's probably waiting to see if I'm stupid enough to show up.

Chapter Seven

"Vince! Vince!"

Someone is smashing on the basement door. I bolt off my bed and drop the video controls on the floor. They're here. They're going to kill me.

"Vince," the voice is panicked. "Open the door, you idiot. Let us in."

It's Nick and Justin. Charlie and the gang are probably right behind them.

I open the door just enough to see what's going on. Nick and Justin are alone. They crowd inside and both start talking at once.

"We were good tonight, man," says Nick. "You should have seen us."

I give them a quick eye scan for bruises and blood. I don't see anything that looks like they've been fighting other than a clump of dirt on Justin's sleeve.

"We were studly men tonight." Justin's slurring his words.

"What are you talking about, man?" I say. "You don't look good for anything."

"Here's the story, man," says Nick. "It was soooo right on." His eyes roll in their sockets. Then he says, "You tell it, Justin."

Justin says, "We're down there waiting under the bridge. We found ourselves a safe hiding spot near the old fence so we could take our time and work out our strategy. Right?"

Then he stops talking. "You tell him, Nick," he says finally. "You're good at stories."

He flops back on the bed. Neither one of them is laughing.

"What's with you guys?" I say. "Just tell me what happened."

Nick coughs and suddenly sounds sober. "Like Justin said, we're behind a bush when they get there. Three cars arrive. We'd already been sitting there long enough for me to pee four times. They pile out. Man, there must have been eight or ten of them and a few girls. They're all puffing joints. They're ripped, man, like right out of their minds. They're laughing and smart-assing around. Charlie shouts your name a few times and the girls laugh like crazies. The girls were talking about plucking your legs."

"All right, Nick," I say. " I don't care what they think of my legs. What happened?"

Nick's thinking hard. "Right. Well they'd only been there a few minutes when Steve arrives with Sherry hanging on his arm. Steve tells them to go home and forget it. And after a while they all pack into their cars and disappear."

"And?" I say. There's something missing in his story.

"And what?" says Nick.

"And what else?" I say.

"Nothing."

"That's not why you were laughing."

"No," he says and hangs his head. "The real story happened after that. Go ahead, Justin. I told the first part. You tell the rest of it."

Justin giggles like a girl and gets this gleeful look in his eyes. He says, "So we

54

scramble out of the bushes and who do we bump into but the chick that's always giving you those cutesy little finger waves."

"Raedawn," says Nick.

"Yeah," slurs Justin. "She's crouched in the bushes just a few feet from where we were. She's been there the whole time."

His eyelids close and he jerks forward like he's falling asleep.

"And?" I say.

His head comes up and he says, "Yeah, so there she is. Looking just as cute as ever. She even gives us one of those sexy looks and says to us, 'Hey guys, what are you up to tonight?'"

Nick lies on his stomach and buries his head in his hands.

"Just like that." Justin wipes his lips and carries on. "You should have heard her. It was like she was giving it away. Right, Nick?"

Nick doesn't move, but I'm instantly raging.

"What are you saying? What was she giving away?"

Justin laughs. "She was giving it all away. Everything, man. You should have heard her. She wanted us." He looks to Nick to back him up. "What are we supposed to do? Say no? We didn't want to disappoint her."

Suddenly Justin gets serious and says, "Then when we're taking our piece, she starts pulling away. She starts shouting at us, telling us to get the hell off her.

"But we got some, right? Both of us. Nick first and then me," Justin says. "You should have been there, buddy. You could have had some too."

I start shaking. "Get out of here," I shout.

"What's wrong with you?" Nick says as he stands up.

"Yeah, Vince," says Justin. "We got some tonight. She'd give it to anyone. No big deal."

"Get out of here!" I holler. "Get the hell out of my house."

I'm ready to explode. They finally stumble out the door. I grab my jacket and throw on my shoes and wait at the door until they're gone. Then I get to the road and race toward the bridge. When I reach the main road at the gas station, I see two cars parked side by side. I creep through the bushes for a few minutes. When the coast is clear, I sprint down the road to the turnoff toward the bridge. At the first sign of headlights coming up the road behind me, I dive into the ditch and wait until the car passes. I scramble to my feet and run onto the bridge.

"Where are you, Raedawn?" I holler up the river on one side of the bridge and out to the ocean on the other.

"Raedawn, can you hear me?"

I stop and listen. Nothing but the sound of my blood pounding. At the end of the bridge, I fall spread-eagled into the bush. I close my eyes until my body stops vibrating. When I open my eyes, I see the fence towering over my head. I'm in the spot that Nick and Justin described. I scramble to my knees and crawl through the bushes to a small clearing. Raedawn was here. This is the place it happened. I'm fuming and suddenly creeped out.

I climb back onto the bridge. I'm too wound up to go home. I veer through the woods to the beach. I remember coming to this place once or twice when I was a kid. Mom had some friends from the city staying in the campsite, and we came down to visit them. Another time our family came to a salmon barbecue. I remember the Indians cooking salmon on spits on the beach and frying bread over a fire. I played in the sand and thought the beach went on forever. As far as I could see there was white sand and surf and driftwood.

When the woods open up onto the sand, the sky is bright but clouds cover the moon and stars. I can see a crescent of sand stretching into the distance. Subtle shades of gray outline the water, sand, massive piles of driftwood and a row of trees that skirt the beach. I start to shiver from the salty damp breeze coming in over the ocean. I throw on my coat and then stand there like I'm waiting for a bus. Gradually, directly over my head, the clouds separate and the moon appears. A column of light shines from the moon across the rumpled water and leads directly to my feet. It's like a pathway to God. I can't move. For an instant, I think God is calling me to this exact spot. I move a few paces to my left and the beam of light follows me. I'm ready to start making promises and spilling my sins, when my brain kicks in.

"Light's going to follow your eye, moron," I say out loud. "And what would God want with you anyway?"

I'm disappointed I don't have some time with God. But suddenly the clouds close together again, shutting out the moon, and the beach looks gloomy and intimidating. I take off toward home, leaving all thoughts of God on the beach.

The lights are on when I get home. Johnny Cash is playing on the stereo. Mom and Dad are in the living room. I have an urge to talk to someone. For a second, I even think about going upstairs and talking to Mom and Dad. What would I say to them? They would never understand the stuff I'm going through. I can just hear Dad flipping out if he heard I wimped out on Charlie. He'd say

I could have taken on the whole gang with one hand tied behind my back. He'd tell me about how he took on a whole gang when he was my age. Mom would have something positive to say. And if I told them I was worried about what happened to Raedawn? Forget it.

She didn't ask for it. She didn't want them. She couldn't have wanted them.

Chapter Eight

Dad's watching golf on TV when I get upstairs in the morning. Mom's flipping pancakes and frying bacon in the kitchen.

"You see Sherry last night?" Dad asks.

"No." I walk into the kitchen. I pick up a slice of bacon from a plate on the counter.

"Do you know where she was last night?" asks Mom.

"Why should I know where Sherry is?" I say, stuffing it in my mouth.

"You and Sherry used to be insepa-rable," she says. "This is a small town. There can't be too many places she could have been."

Dad shuts off the TV.

"Vince, get the hell in here," he says. It doesn't happen very often, so when Dad shuts off the TV, I know he's serious. "I need to talk to you."

"What?" I say sullenly.

"Where the hell were you last night?"

"Playing video games downstairs."

"Where were Justin and Nick?"

"How should I know?"

"Maybe because you and Nick and Justin have spent every Friday night together since you were able to walk."

"Except last night, okay. What's the big deal?"

I'm getting irritated. Why doesn't he just spit it out? Get to the point.

"You want to know the big deal? Sherry's curfew was midnight. Donnie was frantic. She didn't get home until 2:00 AM. She crawled in her bedroom window glassy eyed, staggering and smelling like marijuana."

"Since when is Sherry my problem?" I say. "She doesn't even look at me anymore."

"She said she was with you and Justin and Nick." Dad's eyes are on my face, trying to catch a sign that I had been smoking up.

"So why didn't you come downstairs last night? You could have seen for yourself that I wasn't stoned." I'm still confused.

Mom pipes up from the kitchen. "You weren't home when we first checked. And by 2:00 AM your father was too angry. He'd had a few too many drinks and

I made him promise to sleep it off before he talked to you. I didn't want a row."

A row. That's what Mom calls a fight.

"Yeah, well there wouldn't have been a *row*. I was home all night, except for a few minutes when I went for a walk. I wasn't drinking or smoking up. I don't know what any of them were doing last night. And I don't care."

Mom's voice deepens into her counseling tone. "Vince, you haven't been yourself lately. Is there something wrong? Do you want to talk about something?"

Yeah, I'm thinking, I want to talk about something. I want to tell you that I'm going to get killed by a gang of Indians, that I feel like a chicken because a bunch of freaking girls won't stop teasing me, and I think I'm falling in love with an Indian girl I've never really met.

I think I'm what? How could I be so gross? I'm not falling in love with Raedawn. She's been with Nick *and* Justin. "I don't want to talk about anything, Mom," I say. The truth is, I desperately want to talk to someone who can save me from going out of my mind. That person, however, is not my mom.

Dad hauls himself off the sofa and leans against the kitchen door. He smells of stale beer.

"Let me tell you, Vince," he snarls. "If Sherry's still hanging out with that Indian, Donnie's going to send her into town to live with his sister."

"Whatever," I say. "Sherry can hang out with whoever she wants."

"What did you say?" Dad steps closer.

"I said, mind your own business." All of a sudden I want to stick up for Sherry. "If she wants to hang out with Steve, that's up to her."

"Who the hell is this Steve?" Dad yells. "Some useless Indian thug who sits around smoking dope? I'm shocked to hear that from you, Vince. I raised you different than that."

"Vince," Mom says tightly, "of course we can be friends with everyone, but you know how Donnie and Deb feel about Sherry having an Indian boyfriend."

"Of course I know how they feel. I know how you guys feel as well." I race downstairs and slam my bedroom door.

Chapter Nine

I spend all of Saturday holed up in my room, playing video games and avoiding everyone. On Sunday, when Justin phones, I tell him I'm sick.

I'm not exactly lying. It's true that I feel like puking, but I'm not sick. I just don't want to listen to anyone, see anyone or think about anything. I don't even want to breathe. Yeah, I guess

I am sick. I'm sick of the whole damn world. I shut off my light and lie spread-eagled on the bed. I crank the tunes. Maybe it will drown out my thoughts of Raedawn and my plans to bash Nick's and Justin's heads together.

I hear a faint knocking. I ignore it. When it doesn't stop, I realize that it is coming from the back door. Damn those guys. Don't they get it? I don't want to see them.

The knocking doesn't stop and I get the feeling it's not going to quit. "Who the hell is it?" I shout.

"It's me," a girl's voice says. "Open the door."

My heart lands in my mouth. "Who's me?" I ask. What girl would be knocking on my door on a Sunday evening? Or ever, for that matter.

"Sherry. It's Sherry. Let me in."

I open the door. She looks as if she's waiting for me to get mad.

"Don't just stand there," I say. "Come in."

"Do you mind?" she says.

I want to yell at her. *Why the hell have you been treating me like crap?* I also want to hug her and tell her how much I've missed her. I play dumb and say, "Do I mind what?"

"I mean is it okay that I'm over here?"

She takes one step into the room and stands motionless.

"Sit down," I say and point to her favorite beanbag chair.

She plops into the center and, just as she has done a million times, makes a perfect landing. "Vinny," she says and then starts bawling. Tears spurt from her eyes. "I need to talk to you. You have to help me."

"So you're here because you need my help?" I say.

"No, Vinny, don't take it the wrong way," she sobs. "I'm here because you are my best friend in the whole world and I miss you and I need you. Friends need each other. Even if one of them has been acting like an unforgivable snob."

"Yeah," I say. "You got that right."

"I know, I know. And I am soooo sorry."

Suddenly I realize how much I've missed her. She's the one I've needed to talk to.

She says she's in trouble with her mom and dad. They caught her kissing Steve goodnight and were waiting in her bedroom when she climbed in the window. Now they've decided to send her to the city to live with her aunt and uncle. They're making plans to move her things in a week. Until then she's grounded. No Steve, no friends and maybe even no school. She's allowed over to my house only because Mom and Dad promised them that no one will be allowed in except me.

By now she's crying hysterically. I don't feel like yelling at her anymore. I find a towel and wipe her face. I fumble around the beanbag, trying to get my arms around her. When I finally get a gangly hold of her, a strange thing happens. She's not hot Sherry anymore. She's next-door Sherry with makeup running down her face and snot stuck in her hair.

"Vinny, Vinny," she cries. "You have to help me."

I feel guilty. The whole mess is my fault. I started the flow of information to her mom and dad that led to this disaster. I did want her to get into trouble. I just never thought that it would lead to this.

I try to think of something brilliant to do.

"I love Steve." She's quieter now, but her sobs sound like she's dragging them up from the soles of her feet. "And I love you like my brother. What am I going to do if I have to leave you? We've been side by side since we were born."

"I thought you'd forgotten about me. You dumped me like a hot potato."

"I'm so sorry, Vinny. I was such an ass. I started thinking I was something I wasn't. Guys were looking at me in a way they had never looked before. I thought I was too good for you. I thought I was too good for everyone. You were the only guy who reminded me of who I really was."

"It's okay, Sherry," I say. "We're going to have to talk to our parents." I can't imagine what we will say that would change their minds, but it's all I can think of. "You can't move to town, Sherry. I would miss you. That would be crap."

"What's crap is all that stuff about sticking to your own, and Indians being drunk and stoned and no good for us.

Steve's the best thing in my life. He's the one who called those bozos off you Friday night. He's the one who tells me to do my homework and respect my parents. He's the one who says I shouldn't drink too much." ·

"Yeah, well your parents would never believe that in a million years," I say.

"Then we've got to make them. And in a hurry."

"I'll think of something."

I still feel responsible for getting her problem off the ground in the first place, so I tell her that I'll talk to my parents.

I know it won't do one bit of good. My parents are worse than hers when it comes to prejudice. What I really have in my mind is Raedawn and how much I want to talk to Sherry about her.

"I've got to get home, Vinny. Stinking curfew. We'll talk later. Thank you, thank you, thank you." Sherry lifted both of her palms in the air. "That's how Steve says thanks."

She gets up to leave and then turns around at the door. "Vinny, I haven't told Steve that I'm moving."

"You have to."

"Not yet. We have to think of something to change my parents' minds. Then I won't have to tell him at all."

I can't see the logic in her plan, but what am I going to say? I've messed up her life enough.

Chapter Ten

Monday morning, Sherry and I meet at the bus stop.

"You're here?" I say.

"Mom says I can go to school for one last week," she says. Her eyes fill with tears. "I'm so sad."

"Me too."

It's one thing for Sherry to act like a snob and treat me like crap.

It's another thing to imagine life without her.

I head to the back of the bus, leaving Sherry in her new seat near the middle. Nick and Justin arrive just before the door closes. They saunter down the aisle and plunk their butts on the backseat. They take a look at me and then at each other and start giggling like a couple of girls. "What's so funny?" I ask, wishing they'd shut up.

"That was a good weekend," says Justin. "I haven't had any for a long time."

Nick laughs, but he has sense enough not to say anything.

"What the hell are you talking about?" I say loudly.

"Shut up, Vinny," says Nick. "The whole bus doesn't have to know."

"Why not? If you were so good this weekend, why not tell everyone?"

"Settle down," he says. "We got some. And if you didn't have your head stuck up your butt, you could have got some too."

Justin laughs and says, "Yeah, she would have given everyone some."

At the Indian bus stop, I'm ready to take their teeth out. Then I realize that I don't want Raedawn to hear what's going on. I slump in the seat and wait for her to get on the bus. Steve climbs up, followed by Charlie and his gang.

Charlie shoots a look my way and shouts, "There she is. We were at the bridge, girlfriend, waiting for you. Where were you?" He hoots. "We heard you had to curl your hair."

Laughter erupts. My stomach's turning. I look around for Raedawn. The door closes and she's not in her seat.

Nick and Justin shut up once the bus starts to move. They glance at each other when they realize she's not there.

"Where is she?" I say under my breath.

"Where's who?" says Justin, as if he doesn't know what I'm talking about.

"Forget it."

Monday night, Sherry arrives after supper and hits the beanbag like the night before. Her eyes droop at the corners like a puppy dog looking for a warm place to curl up.

"What are we going to do?" she says. "Mom and Aunt Stephanie are on the phone as we speak. They're making arrangements for the weekend. Saturday, Uncle Dick is coming out with a pickup to take my stuff. Mom and Dad are going to pay them to look after me. Can you imagine, Vinny? It's like I'm being sent to a foster home. For doing what? Nothing. I've done nothing wrong.

"Have you talked to your parents yet?" she asks.

"No." I shake my head. "I'll talk to them today. They'll talk to your parents. Maybe we can get them to change their minds."

"They are best friends." She looks up at me hopefully. This feels like the old days—when I used to rescue her from slippery rocks and high branches. "What are you going to say?"

"I don't know. I'll think of something when I get there. It depends on what kind of mood they're in."

I don't have a clue what I will say to them. The last people in the world I want to talk to are Mom and Dad, and the last subject I want to talk about is Steve and Sherry. I already know what they think.

"They're upstairs, Vinny. Go up and talk to them."

"Not now. I'll talk to them later."

"What good is later?" she pleads. "Time is running out."

"Now?" I ask.

"Yeah, now. That will give your parents time to go over and talk to my parents."

"Now?" I repeat, sounding absolutely dumb.

"Yeah, I'll stay down here and listen to you."

"No, you won't." I might be a pushover, but that's going too far. "If I'm going upstairs to talk to my parents, you're going home. You aren't listening to me."

"Okay, okay," she says, looking disappointed. "You promise to come over and tell me what you said?"

"Yeah. I promise."

She climbs out of the beanbag and runs out the door. I'm left wondering why I said I would talk to them. My mind is blank. I decide to do just what I said—go upstairs and say whatever comes to mind depending on Mom and

Dad's mood. I know it's a stupid idea. They'll never be in the mood to hear what I'm going to say.

When I get upstairs, Dad is watching TV and Mom is reading the newspaper.

"Mom." I clear my throat. "Can I talk to you guys?"

She pulls her glasses off her nose and looks up. "Of course, dear," she says. "Jack, Vinny wants to talk to us."

Dad ignores her and stays glued to the TV.

"Jack," she says again. "Can you turn the TV down? Vinny wants to talk to us."

Dad swivels his head. "Yeah, okay, what do you want?"

"Forget it," I say and turn toward the stairs.

"No," Mom says. "We don't want to forget it. Jack, turn the TV down so we can hear."

Dad grunts and turns the volume down. "I'm listening."

He can hear me now, but I know from his expression that he isn't going to listen to a word I say.

"Sherry's going to move to town," I say. "Did you guys know that?"

"Yeah," Dad says. "So what?"

I feel my ears burning. "So what?" I say. My voice is louder than it needs to be. "So what? It's her life. She's lived in this village all her life. She's gone to school with all of us. She wants to graduate with her friends next year."

"Hell, she'll be pregnant before the year's out if she keeps up with that Indian pothead," he says. "At least this way she'll graduate somewhere."

"How can you say that?" I shout. "You're an idiot."

"Vincent," Mom says, trying to control things. "Don't shout at your father. Deb and Donnie are doing what they think is best for their daughter. It's not our business."

"Oh, so now it's not your business," I say. "You've been on the phone day and night. I've heard you."

Mom says flatly, "We can't change their minds."

"But if you and Dad talk to them," I'm begging now, and I hate it, "won't they at least think again about what they are doing?"

"And what do you expect us to say?" Dad laughs. "Hey, Donnie, it's great that your daughter is hanging around with that pothead? Good for her?"

"Vincent," Mom says as she clears her throat. "We think it's a good idea that Sherry moves away." She pauses. "Before it's too late."

Dad turns back to the TV, ignoring Mom's last comment. "I'm not talking to Donnie. The minute you told me about Sherry and that loser I told Donnie to get his daughter the hell out of this town. Pronto."

I'm furious. I face Dad and holler, "You are a dumbass. Keep thinking like that and you'll lose one of your own kids too."

I turn around and dash down the stairs.

"Vinny," Mom calls after me, "what do you mean?"

"What the hell do you care what I mean?"

I slam the bedroom door. Sherry can wait until tomorrow to hear about my useless effort.

Chapter Eleven

"I was waiting for you to come over last night," Sherry says at the bus stop the next morning.

"Sorry. I was too pissed off to talk. Forget Mom and Dad. They're no help. In fact, they're worse than your parents."

I don't tell her that my dad suggested she move away.

"Then what?" Sherry pleads. "What can we do? How am I going to keep it from Steve?"

"You're not," I say as the bus pulls up. "You better tell him right away, before he hears it from someone else."

At the next stop, Steve gets on. As soon as he sits down, Sherry busts open like a water balloon, tears spurting everywhere. She must be telling him the bad news. As the bus pulls away I scan the seats. Did I miss Raedawn? I stand up and check every head. She's not there.

"What did you do to her?" I snap at Nick.

"We told you, man," he says as he looks around the bus. "She's not here. No point looking for her."

"She wasn't here yesterday either, man," I say, trying not to shout. "She never misses school."

"What of it, man?" he says. "So she's not at school. What's that got to do with us?"

"That's the question, dude," I say. "What's that got to do with you?"

"She wanted us. I'm telling you the truth. Then she pulled away."

"What do you mean she pulled away?"

"Well, after we get started she gets all moral on us and pushes us away." He thinks for a second. "But not very hard."

"What did she say?"

Nick's eyes meet mine. His jaw tightens and his eyes flit around the bus. "Nothing. She just bitched at us, man. So we took it anyway."

He's lying. But I can't tell which part is the lie. Raedawn's not coming to school. That's one thing I know for sure. And Nick and Justin did something to her. I know that as well. And I know that Nick's not cool with his story.

"She was good, dude," Justin chirps up. "And she liked it, right? She really liked it."

"Shut up, man."

I've had enough.

Knock knock knock.

I look at my clock. It's 9:00 Tuesday night.

"Who is it?"

"Open the door," Dad hollers. "Right now."

"All right, all right." I clamber off the bed and unlock the door. "What's your panic?"

Dad and Donnie burst into the room like a couple of firemen. "Where the hell is she?" says Donnie.

I ask, "Are you looking for Sherry?"

"Don't play dumb, Vince," says Dad.

Donnie says, "She didn't come home from school." He looks baffled. "Me and

Deb were at the Raven's Eye having a few drinks with the guys after work. We get home a half an hour ago. Sherry's not home. No sign of her."

I think to myself, *Maybe you should have been looking for your daughter three hours ago.*

"She's probably at Meagan's house," I say.

Dad shouts, "Hell, they've already thought of that. Deb's phoned all Sherry's girlfriends."

Donnie swings around. "I'm going home to get my gun," he blurts out. "You coming with me, Jack? I'm going down to that reserve. I'll find her there."

"Hold on, Donnie," I say. "You don't need a gun. And you're in no shape to be going anywhere."

"I'm Sherry's father…" He sounds like he's got marbles in his mouth.

"Donnie," Dad interrupts. Luckily Dad hasn't had as much to drink as

Donnie. He can see there will be trouble if he doesn't stop his friend. "We'll find Sherry."

"I'll go to the reserve and look for her," I say. "They'll talk to me better than they'll talk to you. Especially considering the shape you're in."

"That's great, Vince." Dad jumps all over my suggestion. "Donnie, let's you and me go to your house, and Vince can go to the reserve and find Steve. Sherry's probably with him."

At the mention of Steve, Donnie almost falls over. "Let me at that son of a bitch."

"Let Vince get your daughter home first," says Dad. "Deal with the pothead later."

Dad looks pleased that for the first time in recent memory we're agreeing with each other. And Donnie's happy that Dad's got it figured out. So it's decided. I'm going to the reserve to find

Sherry. Dad and Donnie walk out and I'm left wondering what just happened.

What have I got myself into? Chicken legs is going to walk straight into the middle of the reserve and offer himself up to Charlie. I'm going to get killed. I know it. I've never been on the reserve before. I don't know anyone who lives there. I don't know where Steve lives. Charlie and his friends might be there. Then I realize I might run into Raedawn. The possibility is all I need to be convinced. I throw on my coat and shoes and head out the door. There are a million stars out, and the moon is so bright I can see almost as well as if it were midday. My lungs sting from the cold air, but I'm pumped with adrenaline. *Raedawn, can I talk to you? I'm sorry for what my friends did. I'm not like them. Really I'm not.*

I cross the bridge and run through a dark stand of cedars that make a corridor along the road leading to the reserve. They're famous old-growth trees that creak and whine like ancient old men when the wind whistles through their branches. Usually I love the forest. I love the way it smells, the air full of living stuff. But tonight I get an eerie feeling that the sooner I get out, the better.

When I reach the reserve road I stop and read a weather-beaten sign that's leaning against a tree. *Indian Reserve. No Trespassing.* I've never imagined walking past the sign and down the road—alone. I can't go back. Raedawn might be there. Before I have time to think too hard, I turn onto the reserve. I walk in the shadow of the trees until I hit a clearing. Suddenly I'm in full view of the reserve. Three roads branch out from a central intersection just up ahead. I can see at least twenty or thirty houses.

Okay, Vince. What did you expect? A sign that said, Steve, This Way? *This is a really stupid idea. How the hell are you going to find anyone?*

I walk down the first road to my right. Kids are having drag races on their bikes like it's Saturday morning. There's a bunch of teenagers on the porch of a house up ahead. Before I have time to take cover and think about what to do, a girl shouts, "Hey, white boy. You lost?"

Now I'm freaking.

This is it.

"No," I shout back. "Or maybe, yes."

Someone throws on a light. They all get a look at me. They explode into fits of laughter.

"It's Chicken Legs. You were supposed to meet Charlie last Friday, under the bridge. You're late, girlfriend."

"This guy really works on Indian time," says someone else.

They laugh and exchange a few more comments about plucking me that I try to ignore. I can't see Charlie, but I recognize a few of his buddies and the girls of course. Who could miss them? As the noise picks up, porch lights turn on up and down the road. I scan the houses, wondering which one belongs to Raedawn.

"I'm Richie, man. What do you want?" A guy comes down the stairs and meets me on the road.

"I'm Vince and I'm looking for Sherry," I say. "She didn't get home from school and her dad's going nuts."

"We know who you are," he says and then turns around. "You see Sherry after school?" he calls to the group on the porch.

"No."

"No."

"No."

"I'm Lucy. You better go see Steve," a girl suggests. "He's the one who's going to know where Sherry is."

"Can you tell me where he lives?"

Lucy points down the road on the other side. Richie leads the way. The rest of the crowd follows.

"So Stevie Wonder has got himself a lady locked up somewhere," Richie says. "Let's go find her."

"He's going to get himself in crap, man," says Lucy. "He should just leave her alone. He doesn't need this."

Richie steps up to the front door of a house painted bright yellow. Even in the dark the place looks like a sunflower. He rings the bell and then stands back.

A huge woman with a mass of thick hair hangs her head out the upstairs window.

"You looking for Steve?" she says.

"Yeah," says Richie. "This guy's here to talk to him."

Without a word she turns around and hollers, "Steve," and then disappears.

Steve appears at the door.

"What the hell is going on?" he says when he sees me. "Is Sherry okay?"

"No, man," I say. "I'm looking for her. Don't you know where she is?"

"Why should I? Last time I saw her she was on the bus."

"She didn't get home from school."

"No way, man. Then where is she?"

"I was hoping you could tell me."

He disappears up the stairs and comes back a second later wearing his jacket.

"I'll find her," he says and brushes past me. Climbing into a car in the driveway, he starts the engine and spins the tires as he takes off. I'm left standing on the porch. Mission accomplished, I'm thinking, but what do I do next?

Richie says, "We'll check down at the beach for you, man. Sometimes white chicks chill out down there."

"Thanks," I say. "I guess I'll check with some of her friends."

"You can find your way home?" Richie says.

"Yeah, no problem. I'm heading back this way." I take off up the road as if I know exactly where I'm going. Richie and the others stay behind, holding a conference in the middle of the road.

I walk slowly, examining each house along the way for signs of Raedawn. Every house has the same windows, same porch and same gravel driveway. Some of the windows have blankets hanging in them, others have beaten-up blinds, but I can see in a few. There are TVs, lights, fridges, stoves—no different than our side of the village. A girl walks toward me on the other side of the road. She's got short legs like Raedawn. But when she gets closer, I can tell it's not her.

"Hi," I say.

"Huh," she mumbles. She looks the other way to make sure I know she's ignoring me.

I start getting confident, like I'm just walking down any old street. Instead of heading back the way I came, I veer onto a short road that cuts across to the main street. All the lights are out in the second house on the right except for the porch light. It looks like no one is home, but then I get a feeling that someone is watching me. I look more closely at the porch and see a girl sitting beside a stack of boxes. She's curled up in a big chair so I can only see part of her outline. I'm sure it's Raedawn.

I slow down and start thinking of something to say. Suddenly the sky explodes and rain starts beating down. I forget my words, and any confidence I had runs down the road with the rain. I throw her a little finger wave, as if

I am waving good-bye from a train. She doesn't move. Thinking she didn't see me, I toss her a full arm wave like I'm directing traffic. She sits like a statue, but I can feel her eyes fixed on me. My brain keeps shouting at me to say hi, but the words are backed up in my throat and I can't spit them out. As I pass the house, I manage to squeak, "Hi."

Unable to stop, I drag my feet to the end of the road. For all I know she is waving her heart out, trying to stop me.

When I finally turn onto the main street, words start falling out of my mouth.

"I'm not one of them, Raedawn. Really I'm not. I'm sorry for what they did." I like the way the words echo in the trees and bounce around with the pelting rain.

"What did you say?" It's the voice of an old man.

I stop in my tracks and look around in the dark. I can't see the guy, but I hear a shuffle coming toward me.

"Nothing. I was just talking to myself."

An old, bent-over guy emerges out of the darkness. He's wearing a plastic rain jacket and hat, and boots up to his knees. He stops when he's opposite me.

"Let me tell you something, son. If you're sorry for something then pick up the bat, step up to the plate and play the ball. It ain't going to do you no good walking down a dark road in the rain talking to yourself for the rest of your life."

He shuffles past me. By the time I turn around, he's gone. My heart's pounding like a jackhammer.

"Step up to the plate. Pick up the bat. Play the ball." I'm a drowned rat, standing on the road, waving my hands and shouting like a lunatic.

Blood's rushing through my body, and for an instant I'm not afraid. I'm ready to run back to Raedawn's house and tell her everything. Then the feeling passes and I take off through the old growth directly to the bridge without stopping.

Chapter Twelve

Just past the gas station a car pulls over in front of me.

Steve sticks his head out the window and says, "Jump in."

"It's okay, man. I'm a puddle. I'll walk home."

Then I see Sherry leaning against him, bawling. I crawl into the backseat.

"She's afraid to go home," Steve says.

"Vince." Sherry's sobbing. I can hear her wiping her nose on her sleeve. "Steve wants to talk to Mom and Dad. There's no way. Tell him it's a bad idea."

What harm can it do? Donnie and Deb are dead set on sending Sherry away anyway.

"It's a good idea," I blurt out.

"Vince!" she wails. "They'll kill me."

"No, they won't. They'll send you to town to live with your aunt. And they're going to do that anyway."

"You're no help at all."

"Yeah, I know. Don't rub it in."

"Thanks, buddy," says Steve. "Maybe they won't hate me so much if they meet me."

"Don't count on that," I say. "But it can't make matters any worse."

"You guys don't know my parents." Sherry's back to wiping her nose on her sleeve.

"Yes, I do," I say. "There's a good chance this won't help. But nothing else has helped either. You got any other suggestions?"

"No," she snivels. "Can you come in with us then?"

"What the hell," I say. "Why not?"

Deb and Donnie look stunned when they open the door. Steve has his arm around Sherry. I'm standing a few feet behind. Before they get over their shock, Steve steps forward and holds out his hand to Donnie.

"My name is Steve," he says as if Donnie doesn't know. "I found Sherry near the river."

When Steve lets go of Donnie's hand, it falls limply to his side. Donnie's mouth is open a crack, but no words come out. Steve gives Sherry a nudge as if it's her turn to speak.

She sets her jaw stubbornly and says in a monotone, "I'm sorry if you were worried about me." She sounds like she's reciting lines in detention.

Deb and Donnie are silent.

"Mr. Porter," Steve says. He steps closer and looks Donnie in the eye. "I'm sorry for any trouble I have caused your family, but Sherry and I like each other. I don't want our relationship to get in the way of her family or her education. But I don't want to stop seeing her either."

Donnie's too busy swallowing his Adam's apple to say anything. Then Steve turns to Deb. He takes her hand and says, "Sherry won't scare you again, Mrs. Porter. Not if I can help it."

Sherry's looking as dumbfounded as her parents are. I'm pretty stunned myself. Steve's totally in charge—the only one out of the five of us with his feet on the ground. I watch in amazement as he steps up to the plate and plays the ball. Donnie and Deb start nodding at him as if maybe they don't hate the ground he walks on.

"That's what we're worried about," Donnie says. "We don't want Sherry missing school and spending all her time with a boy."

"Of course, Mr. Porter," Steve says.

"I was so worried," Deb says.

Steve gives Sherry another nudge.

She says, "I'm sorry, Mom," sounding as unconvincing as she did the first time.

Deb gives her a stiff hug. Donnie mechanically lifts his arm and shakes Steve's hand. I walk home. In a few minutes, I hear Steve's car blasting down the road.

In the morning, Sherry's waiting for me at the bus stop.

"Thanks, Vince," she says.

"For what?"

"For getting Steve last night. And for being there."

"Yeah, no problem. How's it going?"

"Mom and Dad blew a fuse after Steve left. But at least they blame me for everything, not him. It's like nothing's Steve's fault anymore. By the time Mom was finished with me it sounded like she thought I was a bad influence on him."

"Maybe you are."

She punches my arm.

"I'm grounded for a month because I scared the hell out of them. But I don't have to move away. Not this time. And I'm only allowed to see Steve at school. I can live with that."

"Or get around it," I add.

Sherry laughs.

"Sherry," I say. Then I hesitate.

Pick up the bat, you moron.

"Sherry," I say again in case she didn't hear me the first time.

"Yeah."

"Sherry."

"Vince, Vince, Vince." She's laughing at me like I'm an idiot. "You got something stuck in your throat?"

"Yeah. It's been stuck there for a few weeks."

"Then spit it out."

So I tell her. Everything. Ten minutes and she knows the whole story. I'm as good as Mom at telling stories. Once I get into it I can't stop. I tell her stuff I didn't even know myself. I tell her about Nick and Justin. I tell her how Raedawn looked at me and how it feels like an orange is blocking my throat when she says my name. I tell her Raedawn is stuck in my head and I can't think of anything else. I tell her that Raedawn ignored me last night.

The bus pulls up before Sherry has time to say anything. She throws her arms around me and gives me a giant bear hug.

"Geez, Vinny, I would never have guessed. Leave it with me. I'll take care of it."

I fly up the stairs like I'm a bird. Light as a feather, man. It's like a ten-minute conversation lifted a ton of concrete off my shoulders.

Coach Baker is going to be happy with me today. The Hoop Hero has returned. I got the game in my bones. At lunch I race down the hall toward the gym. When I pass the office I see a cop car pulling up in front of the school. I stop and wait to get a look at what's up. A car full of old Indians pulls up behind the cop, followed by a woman driving a pickup. Raedawn is sitting next to her.

I'm going to be late for practice. I back through a doorway and stand behind a bookshelf. I watch the crowd gather in the foyer.

"We're meeting with Principal Chatterton," the police officer says.

"Then we'll find the boys and talk to them," an old Indian woman says. "We will sit together and hear what they have to say."

For a moment I think I should tell Nick and Justin what's going on. Instead I settle back on my heels. Why protect them? This is Raedawn's game. She doesn't need me interfering. When the whole group enters the principal's office, I run for the gym.

"Vince," Coach Baker yells. "You're late."

"Yeah, coach. But I'm all here."

I play solid ball. Mr. Basketball has returned. My blood's flowing like a river.

"You got balls today, Vinny," Coach Baker calls. "What's got into you?"

"I feel good."

I do. Sherry's not moving away, we're friends again, she knows about

Raedawn and justice will be served up to my two former best friends.

I sink a perfect basket from mid-court just as the PA system crackles.

"Vince Hardy to the office."

"What now?" Coach Baker yells. "Get back right away."

"Yes, sir," I say.

Mrs. Chatterton's waiting at the office door with two police officers and an old Indian lady. I scan the place for Raedawn. She's not there.

"Vince, do you know where Nick and Justin are?" Mrs. Chatterton says sternly.

"No," I say.

She sinks one eyebrow and looks at me as if she thinks I'm lying.

"When did you last see them?"

"In math class."

"Are you saying you haven't seen them during lunch?"

"I've been at basketball practice. Nick and Justin didn't show."

"Why?" she asks.

"How should I know?" I say.

"Vince." Her eyes narrow. "This is a serious matter. I don't want you lying for them."

"I wouldn't lie for them," I say.

"Vince," she says firmly, "I'm only going to ask you once more. Where are Nick and Justin?"

"I don't know." No doubt they've seen the police and split. Even she should be able to think of that. "I would tell you if I did."

The old Indian woman looks at me as if she can see the blood pumping through my veins. I bet if I asked her she could tell me how much change I have in my pocket.

"Young man," she says, "do you know why we are looking for Nick and Justin?"

I look her square in the eye and lie. "No, ma'am."

The old lady shakes her head. She says slowly, "We'll talk to this young man later."

"You're dismissed, Vince," Mrs. Chatterton says. "We'll call you when we need you."

Lunch is almost over. I dash out to the parking lot, checking every space for the pickup truck Raedawn arrived in. Gone.

Nick and Justin aren't on the bus after school. Neither is Raedawn. Steve and Sherry haven't showed up yet. Dune's pretty well the only guy sitting down. I flop into the empty seat in front of Dune.

I turn around and just as cool as a cucumber I say, "Hey, man. How's it going?"

"Good. You?" he answers.

"Yeah." I nod like we're old buddies. "Good. I'm good too."

I know it's just a bus seat, but all of a sudden it's like I'm left-handed or rich. It's a whole new thing. I'm sitting in the front of the bus and it's weird. Pretty soon the Indian kids start filling up the seats around me. Richie sits next to me.

Looking like there's never been a seating arrangement, he says, "You guys find Sherry the other night?"

"Yeah," I say. "Thanks."

Once Dune gets off the bus, Sherry and Steve move up behind me and I tell them and Richie what happened at lunch—the police, the old lady, Raedawn. Everything.

When I finish my story, Steve says, "Go down to the beach tonight, Vince. Wait at the campsite office around seven."

Chapter Thirteen

It's still raining that night when I put on a plastic rain jacket and hat and pull on my rubber boots. I hate to do it. I look like an idiot, but there's no other way.

Walking down the road, I'm trying to figure out what Steve has got going on. He said wait at the campsite office, and that's where I'm headed. Steve seems to have stuff under control, and I have a feeling that I ought to find out what he's got planned.

It is black out, and no light reflects off the streams rushing down the road and into the ditches. The river's boiling over its banks.

I walk across the bridge, over the hill and down the path to the campsite office. I slop through puddles the size of small swimming pools. "Steve."

No one could hear me over the surf and river and rain and wind smashing through the woods. I walk to the front of the office and up the stairs to the porch. Underneath a broken canopy that covers the front door there are four or five good feet of shelter.

"Steve." I shake like a wet dog.

I can't see or hear anyone. I swing around to check behind me and I see what appears to be someone curled in a ball by my feet.

"Steve?"

What the hell is he doing? I crouch down and find myself face to face with Raedawn.

"Whoa! Where's Steve?"

"I don't know."

Her voice, like an electric arc, shoots out and grabs my sopping wet body. You know how you think of something over and over and plan exactly what you are going to do? Then when it happens, you forget everything. I'm finally alone with Raedawn and I'm paralyzed.

"What are you doing here?" I ask.

"What are you doing here?"

"Steve told me to come to the campsite office."

"He told me to come here as well," she says.

It's like the storm stops. The place is silent.

"Why?" I say.

"I don't know. Why did he want you to come here?"

"I don't know."

She leans forward to stand up.

"Doesn't look like he's going to show," she says. "I guess I'll go home."

I push myself to a standing position. She's a magnet. The pull is so strong I have to brace myself against the door. I stare at the surf, trying to clear my head. I feel her staring at me and I figure she thinks I'm pretty ugly. She's less than two feet away, looking straight up at me. Finally she looks away and I take a quick glance at her.

"Don't go home," I say.

I snatch a corner of her jacket. She leaps away.

"Let go of me." Her voice sounds like I stuck a needle in her.

I back up a few steps.

"Sorry," I say. "I'm really sorry. I just don't want you to go."

"Why?"

"I want to talk to you."

"You mean you want to lie to me."

"Why do you say that?"

"You lied to my grandmother today. You said you didn't know why they were looking for your two disgusting friends."

"I'm sorry. I really am sorry."

She leans back against the wall. We both wait for the other to speak.

"Are you all right, Raedawn?" I speak first. I'm not positive, but I have a sense that I'm picking up the bat. "I want you to be all right."

"Yeah, well how will I be all right with guys like you and your friends around?"

"I'm not like my friends."

"Yeah, right, Vince. I've lived around here for as long as you. You and those two creeps have hung around since forever. You're like triplets. Seen one, seen them all."

"No, Raedawn," I protest.

"I thought I liked you before Friday night. And then it happened."

"What happened?" I say.

"What do you mean, what happened? Didn't your friends give you the story?"

"Yeah, but I'm not sure whether it's true. I can't believe it."

She bolts backward. "You can't believe it?" she hollers. She's going ballistic on me. "You can't believe it?"

She rolls from side to side on the balls of her feet. "You can't believe your friends would attack me and slobber all over my face? You can't believe they would pin me down and try and rip my clothes off? You can't believe they would call me a slut? What about that can't you understand?"

"Then you didn't want them? And they didn't have sex with you? And you didn't tell them that you liked it?"

"What? What did you say? What did they tell you?"

My arms fly up and wrap themselves around her. Water splashes in our faces. This time she doesn't pull away. She curls into my chest and sobs.

"They said that about me? That's what you think happened?"

"No. That's why I wanted to talk to you."

"Do you believe me?"

Her body goes limp in my arms, so I have to bend down and hold her up. We're so close I can feel her heavy sobs pounding against the thuds of my heart.

"Yeah, I believe you. Their story didn't make sense right from the start. But I didn't know what the real story was. I didn't want to believe them."

I dip my face into her thick black hair. I get a whiff of a mixture of fruity shampoo and a damp musty smell. I want to pick her up and tuck her into my jacket. A cramp tightens up the back of my neck, but I don't move a muscle. The moment might end and it would be all over. She might be thinking the same thing. She stays perfectly still. Seconds turn into minutes. After a while I get a weird feeling. It's like my feet are standing on the ground for the first time in my life. It's like, I'm Vince Hardy and I don't have to be afraid or embarrassed or apologetic. I figure this is how Steve must have felt when he met Sherry's parents. When I get a handle on my new feeling, I squeeze Raedawn a little to test the waters. She moves closer. I nuzzle my face in her hair.

This is home, man. This is where I belong.

For an instant, Mom and Dad flash across my brain. I can see myself standing at the front door with my arm around Raedawn.

"Dad and Mom," I would say, "I'd like you to meet Raedawn."

Nothing else comes to mind. I can't pull up an image of their response. I guess it doesn't matter. I've picked up the bat and hit the ball. I'm in the game and I'm ready to play each ball as it comes.

"My mom's not going to be very happy when I bring a white boy home," Raedawn says.

I laugh. "You've got to be kidding. I was just thinking the same thing about my parents."

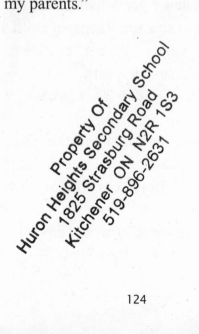